CZARS AND PRESIDENTS

Martha Friesen faced dangers in America
far different from the threat of religious
persecution in her native Russia. Here
there were rattlesnakes, Indians, prairie
fires, and tornadoes. But even more
adventure awaited . . .

Martha learned special lessons from her
neighbors, and Alice, her first non-Mennonite
friend. She and her family survived blizzards
and burning barns. Still there were moments
of great excitement — like the time in
Topeka when President Rutherford B. Hayes
spoke to her! And she'd always be grateful
for Turkey Red. Brought halfway around the
world, it was God's gift that gave them a
new life.

Turkey Red

Esther Loewen Vogt

Illustrated by
Seymour Fleishman

David C. Cook Publishing Co.
ELGIN, ILLINOIS—WESTON, ONTARIO

TURKEY RED

First printing, June 1975.
Second printing, October 1975.
Third printing, April 1976.

Copyright © 1975 David C. Cook Publishing Co.

David C. Cook Publishing Co., Elgin, IL 60120

Printed in the United States of America
Library of Congress Catalog Number: 75-4455

ISBN: 0-912692-68-5

To the Memory of
Grandpa and Grandma Jacob Loewen

Who migrated to America from Russia
as young people around 1874

CONTENTS

1. Terror on the Plains

MARTHA FRIESEN STOOD IN THE DOORWAY of the adobe house and strained her dark eyes to the far horizon. The wide, yellowed prairie stretched out and leaned itself against the sky. Tall grass billowed and dipped in the warm April breeze as Martha closed her eyes. She adjusted her drab scarf carefully over her tawny head and pressed her lips together firmly.

Behind her, Mama's churn thump-thumped the thick sour cream rhythmically. It had gone on for a long time.

Suddenly the churn stopped, and she heard her mother's quick intake of breath.

"Eee, Martha? Aren't you going to take the cold water to Jacob in the field?" Mama chattered in Low German dialect which the Mennonites from the Ukraine still spoke, for it was the year 1877.

"In a minute, Mama," Martha said, flipping one

9

wheat-colored braid with her slender brown fingers. "I wondered if Gerta could go with me."

Mama's thumping began again. "Better you don't wait for Gerta Harms. You know how slow she is. And bossy. Jacob is thirsty. Make sure the water is cold and fresh from the well."

Without a word, Martha grabbed the burlap-covered stone jug from the low bench behind the door and skipped out to the well. The pulley squeaked as she hauled up the big tin pail, laid the cork on the wooden well stoop, and watched as the water gurgled into the narrow jug spout. Plopping the cork back into place, she swung the jug with her left arm and started across the field behind the house.

"I wish I didn't have to go alone," she thought. "The fields are big and the road so long." It wasn't at all like the Ukraine in south Russia where they had lived in the cozy village of Pastwa, with fields right behind each farmstead. Here in Kansas the prairie grass stretched away in endless miles of flat *nothing*. She shook her head. Why had they left Russia to come to Kansas? She would ask Jake when she reached the field.

Her bare toes curled on the hard dry path that skirted one end of the cornfield. Up ahead she heard the *scritch-scritch* of Jake's hoe as he clipped the weeds from the long rows of green corn. His straw hat was pushed back, and a thatch of tangled yellow hair tumbled out. A crease tracked across his red, sunburned face when he saw her.

"What're you doing here, Martha Friesen? You —" He caught sight of the water jug which bobbed against her long, dark blue skirt, and he paused to lean on his hoe. "Well, it's about time you brought me something to drink!"

"Mama said you must be thirsty. Are you very tired?"

"Tired?" He laughed harshly. "Tired and sick of everything. Here we go, leaving our fine, comfortable farms in Russia, and move to this godforsaken country in America called Kansas! What do we have? Nothing. No house, except for the adobe bricks we pour into molds, and dry, and then pile up into walls. Coyotes howling at night. No trees, except for a lone cottonwood or two, and a few young mulberries. No crops but what we scratch into this hard prairie dirt and pray will grow. No friends but those we meet at church — which is nothing but an old run-down immigrant building. Just a bunch of stupid Mennonites who couldn't get along with the Russian government."

He jerked the jug to his lips, pulled the cork, and drew a long draught of fresh, cold water. Martha eyed him in silence. Then she dug her toes into the dust and sighed.

"Jake, just why did we Mennonites come here? Do you know why?"

Jake slammed the jug onto the ground and made a few random scratches with his hoe.

"Well, Martha, it's hard to understand, even for me, and I am 16." He gave a short dry laugh. "You see, the Mennonites, coming from Holland and Germany and Switzerland, had been promised freedom of worship and freedom from serving in the Russian army if they settled in the rich, fertile Ukraine Valley. Once Count Leo Tolstoy visited us. We were *somebody* there. But the leaders who came into power changed their minds. I guess some Mennonites were growing rich, and the Russian leaders didn't like that. Why should the Mennonites have everything? So the czars got a mite tough, and what did our parents do? Chucked all their good living aside and came to America. *Now we are nobody.* Here in Kansas the good farms you see are the homes of soldiers who once fought in the Civil War. They used their mustering-out pay to help buy them. The shacks belong to the Mennonites. The government owns every other section along the Santa Fe Railway right-of-way, and the sections between these are the ones the railroad is now offering to us Russian Mennonites, especially those from our Molotschna colony in the Ukraine. Why? Maybe because we are hard-working. We have learned to work together."

He scowled and shook his head. *"Ach,* we might all have lived in New York City and got jobs and become rich there. But now. What did we do?" He paused again and laughed bitterly.

"What did we do?" Martha echoed quietly, waiting for him to go on.

"Like I said, Mennonites must stick together! So our fathers bought land — tall, grass-bound prairie land. Here, away from everyone. Well, I've had it. One of these days —"

"One of these days — what, Jake?" Martha prodded.

"Jake Friesen doesn't have to live here, grubbing out his papa's crops with his bare hands. Look at that wheat over there — Turkey Red — acres and acres of it. Know what it takes to harvest it, Martha?"

"Papa scythes and ties it into bundles —"

12

"And threshes it with the threshing stone! There are easier ways to make a living. In the city."

Martha wet her lips with her tongue. "But Papa is a good farmer. All Mennonites are! All this land —" She made a sweeping motion with her hand to the wide fields of wheat and the long, straight rows of green corn.

"Indians. And rattlesnakes. Be careful of them, Martha. They can be terrifying," Jake said bluntly. He grabbed the jug and took another swig of water from the spout.

"The Indians or rattlesnakes?" Martha asked, her dark eyes wide.

"Both. That's another reason I want to get away. There's no need to surround oneself with danger. Oh, sure. Indians can be friends, too — if they wish. They live close to nature and they know about — things. But white men took their land away. Now we'd better watch out!"

For a moment Martha stared at her brother. Then she picked up the jug. "I guess I'd better go back, Jake," she said.

"Sure. But better be careful. And don't forget what I said."

She hesitated, then swung around and started down the dusty path again. She couldn't understand Jake. He seemed sullen and unhappy. He had always been such a happy person until they came to America. Was it true they had left the good life behind in Russia in order to settle in this lonely, wild new land, as Jake had said? Maybe she didn't understand it, but hadn't Papa and the other church leaders prayed about it? And hadn't God led them here?

She shuffled through the thick dust and watched it curl between her toes. Sweat poured over her neck and she stopped and whipped off her kerchief. Why did little Mennonite girls wear these drab three-cornered scarves that didn't keep off the hot sun while prim English-speaking girls covered their faces with pretty slat sunbonnets?

A sudden whirring sound beside her caught her attention. What was that? It sounded eerie, like the voice of evil.

Then she saw it: an angry snake, coiled and ready to strike. She froze. What could she do? She was terrified. Jake was right, after all. Now she could only wait until the snake sank its fangs into her bare leg.

2. Enter: Gray Fox

"HOLD STILL, WHITE GIRL!"

A low, husky voice spoke behind her. Slowly she turned.

A tall slender Indian stood beside her. His jet black hair was kept in place by a leather thong, his strong bronze face slashed with a white smile and his forehead by heavy brows. He wore a long red tunic and dun-colored trousers. Martha wanted to scream, but her voice stuck in her throat.

Panic-stricken, she watched the Indian take aim with a thin whiplike strip of hide, and with a swift, sharp thrust, slice the rattler's head from its body. The snake twisted and writhed wildly for a few minutes and then lay still.

Martha opened her mouth to mumble thank you, but the Indian stared at her with steely black eyes, whirled around, and disappeared behind a clump of wild plum bushes.

15

Her legs trembling, Martha moved slowly down the path. The jug in her hand shook, and she knew it was the fear which did it. She was almost too numb to think.

After what seemed like a long time, she stumbled across the sandy yard and burst breathlessly into the adobe house.

Mama, busily slapping butter into wooden molds, looked up from the oilcloth-covered table.

"Martha? What is wrong? You look frightened."

Martha flung herself on the low, quilt-covered settee and covered her face with her dark blue apron.

"Ach, Mama!" She gasped out the words. "Jake was right. The rattlesnake — and the Indian —"

"Eee? Now what?" Mama said sharply. "You go a little ways into the field to bring water to your thirsty brother and right away you —"

"I didn't — want to go — alone," Martha sobbed. "I wanted Gerta to go with me. Maybe I wouldn't have been so afraid."

"Afraid? Of what?"

"Mama, if we had stayed in Russia we wouldn't have to be scared. Jake says —"

"Your brother Jacob is not happy with our move to America. He doesn't know what he's saying," Mama interrupted, giving the table a quick swipe with a gray rag. "What's he been telling you?"

"About — about snakes, rattlesnakes and — and Indians. On my way home, Mama, there was an awful snake just ready to strike. But then an Indian was there and chopped the snake's head off. Just like that!"

Mama smiled wryly. "Just like that, eee? Jacob

talked your head so full of fears, you see snakes and Indians!"

"I really did, Mama! Jake said —"

"Jacob doesn't know what he is saying. Don't forget that. I want you to go to the garden and pick peas. They are ready for making soup. And no more snakes and Indians, Martha," she added in her no-nonsense voice.

Slowly Martha raised herself and straightened her drab scarf. She picked up a small enameled pail from the kitchen shelf and stepped outside. Beyond the house near the water trough Mama had planted rows of peas, beans, radishes, onions, lettuce, and cabbages. Now the peas were ready.

She stooped over the straight long rows, picked up the fat green pods, and plunked them into the pail.

While they had lived in the Ukraine she had made Mama's vegetable garden her special project. She had planted and hoed and watered, always basking in the cool shade of the wide elms and mulberry trees clustered in the yard of the pleasant village of Pastwa. But here the plains lay hot and motionless under endless blue skies, and there was so much space. Was Jake right, after all? Did too much danger lurk in Kansas? Mama didn't think so. Mama didn't even believe about the Indian and the snake.

"She won't believe either if I tell her Jake wants to go away. No, I won't tell anyone. We'll see who's right. And I didn't imagine the Indian and the snake!"

With that, she eyed her pail with a satisfied smile, picked it up from the ground, and shuffled across the yard to the house.

3. Tinsley's Store

MAY CHERRIES HUNG PLUMP AND PINK from the young trees for the first time since they were planted when the Friesens had settled with other Mennonite immigrants in Kansas in 1876. Each evening, when the sweet warm air cooled with late afternoon shadows, Martha helped strip the ripe fruit from the low branches.

One morning after cherries had bubbled merrily in the big iron kettle on the stove, Mama spooned them carefully into clean glass jars which she sealed tightly. Then she wiped her cheeks with one corner of her gray-checked apron.

"Martha," Mama said, "I want you to go to Tinsley's store for more sugar. The cherries are sour, and if I don't sugar them a little they won't taste right. Tell Mr. Tinsley we will pay when the wheat crop is harvested."

Martha glanced up from the huge dishpan which was full of cherries she was stemming. "Can Gerta go with me this time? Please?"

Mama paused with a ladle in her hand. "Ach, it takes longer when two giggly girls go together. But if you promise to come home right away, yes, she can go with you. If her mama agrees."

Jumping up fast, Martha almost upset the pan of freshly stemmed cherries. She flew into the corner for her kerchief. The store was a little more than half a mile down the road, and Gerta lived on the very next farm.

"We'll hurry, Mama!" she called over her shoulder as she sped down the long wagon-rutted lane. The dusty road was hot, but anything was better than crouching over the big pans of cherries in the stifling kitchen.

Minutes later she raced up the narrow drive that led to the Harms' A-shaped farmhouse. Gerta had just finished the dinner dishes and was hanging wet tea towels on the line outside.

"Gerta, can you come with me to Tinsleys' store? Mama needs sugar to can cherries," Martha said.

Gerta's black eyes blazed. "Just to get sugar. What's wrong with molasses? But wait, I'll run in and ask." Her long, blue-black braids bobbed on her scrawny neck as she slammed into the house.

Seconds later Gerta was back. "Mama says if we hurry I can go. She needs me to hoe the garden. It seems all our families think about is food," she added with a short laugh.

"If we don't get rain soon, we won't raise much to eat," Martha said. "So Papa says."

The two girls swung down the road and headed east. Tinsley was a Civil War veteran who had had first chance at the land with his mustering-out pay from the army. He had opened a country store near the road on his property several years ago.

Martha loved the smell of spices and drying apples and ground coffee and pickles in the open barrels in the store, although the Mennonites never seemed to have money to buy anything more than what they had to have.

As the two girls entered breathlessly, Mr. Tinsley was very busy with Mr. Becker who was buying supplies for a move to Canada.

A slim, golden-haired girl, in a pink full-skirted gingham dress with short puffed sleeves, danced toward the two girls.

"Hello! I'm Alice Tinsley. My father's busy just now. Can you wait?"

Martha and Gerta looked at each other. They couldn't understand English too well.

"Yah, I t'ink we can wait," Martha said slowly. "If it does not take so very long. I'm Mart'a and this is Gerta."

"We are neighbors," Gerta added brusquely. "And best friends!"

Alice smiled brightly. "Well, why not come with me to the house until my father is ready for you? I think we should learn to know each other. We might become friends, too."

She started out the side door and Martha followed. She beckoned to Gerta to come. Gerta looked at her with a question in her black eyes.

"She's not a Mennonite," she mumbled in Low

21

German. "So she can't be our friend. Don't forget that, Martha."

"Ach, we have to wait anyhow, so we might as well see where Alice lives," Martha said. Gerta always thought she knew best.

The cindered path that ran to the white frame house was ablaze with a border of gay pinks and tall violet larkspur. Alice opened the door and the two girls followed her into the roomy kitchen. White muslin curtains stirred at the open windows, and a Seth Thomas clock on a shelf ticked loudly. The walls were covered with flowered wallpaper, and a cool blue-checked linoleum covered the floor.

Martha drew in her breath sharply. This was a real home. Not mud-plastered walls and a bare, wide-board floor. Wouldn't it be wonderful to live in a big white house with at least four rooms like this, and real wallpaper covering the walls? And a bright carpet on the floor?

Gerta was quiet for a change. She had hardly bossed all afternoon. Maybe she was impressed, too.

Alice motioned to the table. "Let's sit down and get to know each other. How do you like Kansas by now? Have you gotten used to the everlasting wind? I understand the county plans to build a schoolhouse over on the hill yonder." She waved her hand toward the eastern horizon. "And we'll all go to the same school. Wouldn't that be nice?"

Martha gulped at the idea. "We will learn everything English then? I don't know if Papa —"

"Why, this is America, Martha. Surely you don't expect to speak your Low German the rest of your lives."

22

"We — we are Mennonites," Gerta protested thickly. "We don't need to do everything — like — like you do. We stick together!"

"But, why? Why can't you learn from us, and we from you?" Alice asked. "Martha, why should we be so different from each other?"

Martha shook her head solemnly. It was something she couldn't understand. Papa always said the Mennonites must "keep separate." Papa again. Jake said Papa didn't know everything, either. But the Mennonites had God on their side, didn't they? Papa said so. She glanced around hastily. There wasn't even a Bible in the pleasant Tinsley kitchen.

Alice bubbled with questions. "Why do you girls wear such dark dresses and kerchiefs? Why can't you wear pretty gowns and frilly bonnets? Here, let me show you." She rushed into the dark, cool bedroom and returned promptly with a long, pink silk dress. A full ruffle of lace neatly edged the neckline, and matching rows of lace marched down the front of the full skirt.

Martha gasped. The dress was beautiful! She had never seen anything as lovely as this! Gerta's black eyes snapped in surprise.

"Ach, how nice!" Martha whispered. "I wish I — but no — we Mennonites do not believe in worldly things. We —"

"Put it away!" Gerta growled. "We don't believe in temptation."

Alice's blue eyes looked hurt. "But, what's wrong with pretty things?"

Before Martha could think up an answer in English, a small tousle-haired boy wandered into the

24

kitchen. His cheeks were flushed and red from sleep, and a heat rash covered his face and arms. He walked over to a glass bowl and helped himself to several pieces of hard rock candy. Then he plodded to the girls and offered a piece to each of them.

Alice spoke up. "This is my brother Willis. He's six years old. Better get back to bed, Willis. You're sick. Well, girls, maybe my father is ready to wait on you now. Shall we see?"

She flung the pink dress carelessly over the back of a chair and started for the door, and the two girls followed meekly. The candy crunched ever so lightly in Martha's mouth and she savored the sweet flavor for as long as she could. She noticed that Gerta's yearning eyes lighted on the dress, and then they hardened.

"How wonderful it must be to live in a fine house, wear silk dresses, and eat store candy any time," she thought. But that wasn't the Mennonite way, she scolded herself. Her parents knew best. She must believe that.

4. The Cloud

"MARTHA, I WANT YOU TO GO WITH JACOB and pick blackberries down by the creek," Mama said a day or so later, scurrying around in the kitchen with buckets and pans.

"Ach, Mama, it's so hot. I don't see —"

"It will be cooler under the trees. I must have the berries while they are dark and sweet to make into jams and jellies. Think of the good thick spread you can put on fresh home-baked bread next winter."

"Or the blackberry wine we can drink by the fireside," Jake added with a sly wink.

"Eee, Jacob, you are thinking wicked again!" Mama chided. "God will not bless us if we are drunk with wine."

Jake looked at Martha and shook his head helplessly. She knew what he was thinking: "God isn't blessing us now either, even if we act holy and pious

27

and never take a drink at all." He'd said it so many times.

"Yes, Mama," he muttered with a patient sigh. Sweat beaded his forehead and ran in trickles down his red face, and Martha watched him anxiously. Jake was her dear brother — her only brother; yet, lately he sometimes acted like a stranger. He had never wanted to leave Russia and its comfortable village life, and now he was like a calf tied up in the pen, trying to break loose.

The air lay hot and still like a thick band around the world, and brown sparrows chirped listlessly in the brush along the fencerows. Martha grabbed her kerchief from its nail behind the door and tied it under her chin.

She followed Jake out of the house, carrying a tin pail in each hand. She watched as Jake flung the battered saddle on Prince's back, for they were to ride the old horse to the Cottonwood Creek a mile away.

Prince clop-clopped slowly down the pasture path and made his way tiredly toward the creek. Black clouds smudged the horizon and pressed down firmly on the prairie. Even the thick shade along the creek seemed to smother them as they reached the water. Where the creek backed up around a triangle of logs and moss-shouldered rocks, the water formed a quiet little pool. Water striders skated back and forth on the still water, and sunlight made warm freckles of light everywhere, slanting down through a tangle of elms and cottonwoods.

Martha began to pick the luscious black fruit from the prickly bramble near the creek as Jake tied Prince to a cottonwood tree.

She plopped the ripest, most purple berries into her mouth and watched the juice stain her rough brown fingers. A restlessness gripped her as she glanced sideways at her brother. Jake was silent as he plunked plump berries into his pail. His chin jutted out stubbornly and he pressed his lips into a firm gray line. Something was bothering him and she wished she knew what it was.

"Dratted thorns!" Jake growled, sticking his thumb into his mouth.

"Jake, you said a bad word! You know Papa wouldn't —"

"No, Papa wouldn't like it because Papa thinks all Mennonites are Christians and that only his way is right! Here we are, tearing our fingers in order to scrape together a few measly berries so Mama can cook jam. Well, at Pastwa we had bees and honey and fruit trees. We had plenty to eat. We didn't have to squeeze our food from stone-hard prairies and thorny bushes!"

"But God led us —"

"God!" Jake flung out the word bitterly. "Sometimes I don't even believe in God. Why did He lead us here?"

"Papa and Mama have always taught us to believe in God. Maybe they know more about Him than we think."

"Look, Martha. They're a pair of wonderful people. Don't get me wrong. But they have been so carried away about being Mennonite that they won't let us become what we want, or do what we want to do. They'll never change. Either we do as they wish, or — out!"

"If God showed He was more powerful than the Mennonites, would you believe then?" Martha asked in a tight voice.

He spread out his purple-stained hands. "Depends."

"Ach, Jake, I'm sorry you feel that way. I thought maybe —" The words died in her throat, for a nameless fear gripped her. The bank of gray clouds had suddenly boiled up into a greenish-gray mass, and the air had grown stagnant and breathless. The birds stopped their aimless twittering as the greenish clouds whipped themselves into a bowl that grew long and twisted and black.

Martha's hands froze on her bucket as she watched in horror. "Jake, we'd better run for shelter!"

Instantly Jake dropped his pail and grabbed her hand. Together they raced for the dry stream bed nearby, and he flung her down on the ground and threw himself beside her.

"What is it?" Martha whispered.

Jake's jaw muscles worked back and forth. "I think it's a storm cloud — a — a tornado!"

The goblet-shaped cloud touched the far end of the horizon, poised for a moment, swayed dizzily, then moved steadily across the open prairie. Now it grew restless and charged over the fields with a maddening roar. The whole world cowered silently, except for the center of the great black bowl that moved swiftly across the face of the earth, sweeping everything into its maw. Once the stem stretched and pulled away from the bowl, but it did not break. Then it moved wildly, crazily, toward the ditch, and reached out for the two of them.

Martha clung to Jake's neck, closed her eyes, and waited in terror. "God. . . ." God was speaking through the cloud, and she couldn't understand.

Jake swallowed hard, but he didn't say a word.

At last the glass shattered and the bowl broke slowly, splintered into small pieces, and fell apart. Then it rolled itself in thick gray-black smoke over the fields.

She stole a glance at her brother. His face was stony and hard as ever. He hadn't seen God in the storm as she had. Or maybe he hadn't wanted to.

He grabbed her hand and pulled her to her feet, and together they ran to pick up the buckets. He whistled for Prince, who trotted up behind them, wild-eyed. Soon it would rain and they must hurry home. Uprooted trees were everywhere, and the tall prairie grass lay flattened.

Martha was sad. Not because of the storm, but something about Jake was very wrong. She didn't know what it was, and she was even more frightened than when she had seen the rattlesnake. She wanted Jake to be full of laughter and funny stories and comfort, the way he used to be. But he was stern and quiet. The cloud had come with fury, and then it slipped away, leaving only upturned trees and flattened grass. But Martha's heart was still heavy, as though the cloud was still there.

5. Where Is Jake?

SEVERAL DAYS LATER Martha tumbled out of bed in the loft and crept downstairs. Mama sat quietly at the large homemade table, her elbows propped up, and tears in her gray eyes. There was no sign of Papa or Jake.

"What is the matter, Mama?" Martha asked, troubled at her mother's sorrowful face.

Mama drummed her work-worn fingers idly on the oilcloth. "Martha, this morning your brother Jacob is gone. He — he left a note."

Martha drew back sharply. So Jake had done what he said he would do. Somehow she wasn't surprised. She knew someday it would happen. Picking up the folded, ruled scrap of tablet paper which lay on the table, she read in Jake's faltering German script:

"I am going away. I do not like the dangers, the hard work, the loneliness, and never having enough money. Perhaps someday — after I have made it good — I will come back. But don't wait for me. Jacob."

Martha folded the paper and laid it on the table again. "Jake told me he was going to run away. I thought he was only joking." Tears stung her eyes.

"Joking!" Mama gasped. "But why didn't you tell us? We had no idea —"

"Tell you?" Martha blurted out. "You wouldn't believe me about the Indian and the rattlesnake. I didn't think you would believe about Jake."

Mama shook her wispy-haired head stonily. "Eee, this country is all so new, and there is much to learn. We didn't know Jacob felt this way. Or that he was serious about the way he did feel. But we will pray. Our dear Heavenly Father will bring Jacob back to us. We must believe that."

Martha was silent. She had heard too much of Jake's grumbling to believe it would be soon. Papa needed Jake to help in the fields, so it would be hard for him to be patient. And Mama was always fluttering over him like a mother hen with her baby chicks. To Martha, Jake was a friend, a wise older brother who liked to tease and tell stories. But since the tornado Jake hadn't been the same. She would miss him most of all.

A few days later Martha awoke with a hot, feverish feeling in her head. A dry, hacking cough tore at her throat, and she lolled listlessly in her bed. A rash of red spots peppered her neck, spreading slowly over her body, and she began to feel miserable.

Mama hovered over her, bathing her hot face with cool water from the well.

"Martha, Martha, where did you pick up this case of measles? No one in church has come down with them!"

Somehow, somewhere a faint memory stirred in Martha's mind. A plump, sticky little boy with heat rash — or could it have been measles? He offered her a piece of hard rock candy. Alice Tinsley's brother Willis.

She tried to tell Mama now, but it was so hard to talk. The words stuck in her throat and she couldn't get them out. The hot wind blew through the open windows and scorched her flaming cheeks. Her lips grew dry and chapped, and she moaned because she felt so miserable.

She wished suddenly for Jake — Jake who could tell her funny stories and make her laugh. Who would tell her she looked as though someone had splattered red paint all over her? But Jake was gone, and Jake wouldn't come back for a long, long time.

"Jake, Jake, I — want — you. I need you, Jake," she cried, trying to raise herself on her elbows. "Where are you, Jake? Come — come here. The — the cloud. It's coming. God — is bigger than the — the c-c-cloud. . . ."

Mama pushed her back gently and placed a cool hand over her hot forehead.

"Martha, Martha," she soothed, "lie back and don't worry. Jacob would come if he could, if he knew you were sick and needed him. God will bring him back someday. But now —"

"You — you were right, Jake, about the dangers," Martha mumbled. "The snakes and Indians. . . ." She closed her eyes wearily. It was all so dark and hot and weird, like the cloud, and she felt awful. She pushed away the tin cup of cold water Mama had drawn from the well. She wanted only to shut everything out, to forget the wild prairies with their terrors and remember, as Jake did, the lovely fruitful life they had left behind. The wide, sunlit valleys, the clusters of grapes in the vineyards, the lush pastures. But she knew it was gone forever. Would Jake ever return?

6. Wheat Harvest

JULY WINDS HAD WHISTLED HOT AND DRY across the prairies for days, it seemed. Ever since the dead of winter and through the early spring the wind had blown, whipping the fine dust from the bare fields which had been turned by plow with oxteam and horses. The everlasting Kansas wind, as Alice had called it. But now it had blown itself out and stopped.

Martha came out of the house and sauntered toward the well, her drab kerchief pulled over her hair just above her forehead. How she wished for a sunbonnet like Alice Tinsley's! She squinted at the pale, hot sky and glanced at the Harms' wheat field across the road. It was dead ripe, and farmers were swinging their scythes to mow down the fat-kerneled stalks which farm boys tied into bundles.

She sighed. Papa had struggled to finish cutting wheat on their own acres beyond the house, clipping away at the vast field which seemed endless. And Jake should have been there helping Papa harvest.

The heat flickered down from a bare sky as from an overhead oven, cooking the world.

"At least the wind has let up." Martha mumbled to herself. She drew up a bucket of cold water and poured it into the burlap-covered stone jug until it gurgled out of the spout. Replacing the cork, she picked it up and set out across the field. It was time to take Mr. Enns and Papa a drink of fresh water.

The worn path that crawled along the wooden fence bore deep cracks, and the dry thistles plucked at her bare ankles as she sped along the edge of the land.

As she panted toward the north end of the field she saw the wheat was all cut, and Papa was helping Mr. Enns capably tie it into neat bundles. Next these bundles would be loaded onto racks and taken to the threshing floor across from Tinsleys' store.

The wheat kernels looked red and plump, and Martha was sure they would have a good harvest. She remembered how they had brought wheat seed of the hard winter variety from Russia. First grown in Turkey, the reddish kernels were known as Turkey Red, the finest wheat in the world, Papa said. It made wonderful bread, and there was nothing like the crusty brown loaves Mama baked in the long Russian oven. At least they still had their oven.

Papa waved at her and shouted from a distance. "Here comes our water girl with a fresh cold drink! Martha, you haven't melted from the hot sun?"

She hurried through the newly cut field, her bare feet being pricked by the sharp stubble and kicking up wisps of dust.

"Ach, Papa, if only I had a sunbonnet like Alice Tinsley's. Hers is pink, but I wouldn't mind if mine was gray."

Papa took a long, deep draught of water from the jug and laughed. "If Mama has some leftover apron scraps, tell her to see if she can cut a paper pattern from Mrs. Tinsley's. I think it's time you had something to keep off the hot sun." He placed an arm around Martha's shoulder and together they walked over to the shade of a wild plum bush and sat down. "Come, Enns," he called, "it's time for a bit of rest."

Mr. Enns pushed his straw hat back from his sunburned forehead, picked up the jug, and drank.

"Soon we are done binding the wheat, and then it's threshing time. Did you know there is a machine which cuts wheat and another one which threshes it, Martha?"

"Oh!" Martha gasped. "You mean wheat can be threshed without rolling the stone over the stalks? Wouldn't it be wonderful to own one of those machines?"

Papa took off his hat and scratched his balding head. "Nice, yes. But those machines cost money! Yes, it would be wonderful — if we could afford one."

"Jake would like that," Martha murmured. "If Jake thought we'd get one, maybe he would come back."

"Jacob looks for the easy life," Papa said sternly, "and life for the Mennonite farmer is never easy. Or without danger."

"Our Lord never promised an easy life in this world," Mr. Enns intoned solemnly.

"Why did He permit some people to get rich without working so hard?" Martha blurted out. "Jake always said —"

Papa looked at her gravely. "Martha, Martha, have you no respect for your elders? We are doing it God's way. Not Jacob's!"

Papa would never admit he was wrong, or that maybe Jake was right.

She jumped up, retrieved the jug, and said, "I had better get back to the house. Mama will want me to carry water to the garden before I begin the chores."

She made her way back along the narrow path on the hard-packed dirt that led to the farm. She thought again of Jake and that he had not been home to help with the harvest this year. She wondered if he was happy where he had gone. But of course he would be. She knew how hard it was to cut the acres and acres of wheat with a scythe and sickle and to bind it all by hand, and then to roll the heavy threshing stone over the heads of wheat to beat out the firm red kernels.

"The Tinsleys and other English neighbors must think we Mennonites are stupid and backward," she mumbled to herself, "to harvest our wheat like this. And our clothes — drab brown and dark blue and gray. Are Mennonites really stupid? Still, Papa says I can have a sunbonnet!"

She lilted a little with the thought. Well, maybe they were poor, hard-working, old-fashioned Mennonites who were always destined to have a hard life because God had never promised them an easy life, as Mr. Enns said. If only Jake would come back it would be easier. She missed him so.

When she came around the north side of the house she felt the cool moist earth of the newly planted hollyhocks under her feet. Tears welled up in her throat. If only things would be different someday. Tall trees around the house instead of prairie grass, cattle grazing in the pastures, chickens scratching in their pens, and above all, Jake's happy laughter in the background again.

Opening the screen door, Martha hurried into the kitchen. The bare plank floor felt cool under her hot feet. Gerta jumped up from a low footstool and flew to meet her.

"Martha, we are threshing today, and guess what? Mr. Tinsley says he has never seen finer wheat than our Turkey Red! He wants to bring in a thresher for next year, a machine that will thresh the kernels from out of the straw. We won't need the threshing stone much longer."

"Yes, Papa talked about it this afternoon. That would be great!"

"But is it right to make things easy?" Gerta asked.

"Right?" Martha echoed. "Why shouldn't it be right? If our Turkey Red wheat is so good —"

Turkey Red wheat good? But, of course, Papa always said the hard wheat made the best bread. The aroma of Mama's freshly baked loaves still clung to the mild afternoon air, and that was proof!

7. Cousin Ben

SEPTEMBER TRIPPED IN like an Indian princess, gowned in her tawny prairie robes with a gay band of wild yellow sunflowers and purple ironweed tangled in her hair.

School would open in two more weeks, and Martha looked forward to attending the sod schoolhouse again where she was learning to read and write and also to speak the English language.

Papa had been busy turning sod with the one-share plow for next year's wheat crop. Hard winter wheat was always planted in the fall, and after this past year's good crop they would sow more than usual.

Mr. Tinsley and the other English-speaking neighbors had always raised spring wheat, which was only now ripening and ready for harvest. No wonder they eyed the Mennonite Turkey Red fields with surprise.

Martha sat on the low stone wall that fenced in the

vegetable garden and looked across the level fields. Although the sweet corn had stopped bearing, fresh tomatoes and peppers still grew lush and plump on the bushes inside the wall.

"If I hadn't carried water from the well for them all these weeks. . . ." She pondered as she pushed the pink sunbonnet from her hair. It had been such a dry summer and, without Jake's help, it was harder than usual. But now the hot, dry, windy days had gone, the heavy work had lessened, and there was more time. Martha looked forward to school and also to her cousin Ben's coming.

Ben Goertz and his parents, Eli and Anna, and Ben's little sister Tina had left the Ukraine six weeks ago and were on their way to Kansas right now. Ben was a year older than Martha, but they had always played together while they lived in Pastwa and were the best of cousins. Aunt Anna was Mama's sister and, since there was no other place to go, they would stay with the Friesens for awhile.

For days Mama had baked and scrubbed and cooked and cleaned, so the whole place was spotless; even the garden was free of weeds.

Martha toyed with the wide strings of her sunbonnet — Mrs. Tinsley had offered a scrap of plain pink percale along with the newspaper pattern — and wiggled her bare toes in the dirt along the fencerow. It wouldn't be easy to explain to Ben about the flat prairie land, the adobe bricked two-room house with its crude, homemade furniture, the far-apart farms, the bad cloud, the rattlesnakes. . . . She shivered a little. If Jake were here, he could tell it all so much better.

The sound of creaking wagon wheels and the sound of prancing horses broke into Martha's thoughts, and she jammed her bonnet back over her hair and looked down the road. The wagon slowed and then turned into the deep-rutted drive. Was it Cousin Ben and his family already?

Jumping from the stone fence, Martha flew toward the house. The creaking had stopped and Ben sprang to the ground. Martha threw her arms around his neck, then stepped back a little and looked at him with a smile.

"Ach, Ben, you have grown so! But it's good to see you."

Ben grinned. His stubborn lock of hair still fell into his dark blue eyes, and his nose seemed more freckled than ever. Tina, at six, was as tiny and blonde and frail as Martha remembered her. Her long brown dress made her seem even more so.

Amid the chatter of excited voices, the Goertz family soon settled into the adobe house. Ben and Tina eyed the adobe bricks curiously.

"We'll be staying with you while our papa goes farther north to look for land to buy," Ben said after Martha had led the way to the newly planted mulberry grove. "Everything's so vast — so big and wide here. I hope I'll like this new land. It — it —"

"Ach, you have to get used to it. Or so Mama says. And God led us here, Papa says. So it must be right," Martha said.

Ben looked at her intently. "But you're not so sure, are you? *Hui,* you wear a sunbonnet, Martha? Like the English girls?"

Martha laughed. "A bonnet keeps off the hot sun.

Things are always happening here. Like — like meeting an Indian and seeing a rattlesnake."

"Indians? There are Indians around?"

"They live on the reservation, but they come here to hunt and fish. We have a friend named Gray Fox. At least, that's what Papa says he is!"

"Well, I guess I won't be afraid then. Anyone else nearby?"

"We have good neighbors down the road. Alice Tinsley lives east of here. The Tinsleys own the neighborhood store."

Ben's blue eyes lit up. "A store, eh? Look, here are a few pennies. Papa gave me some for selling our horses for him back in Russia. Can we go to the store so I can buy a bit of candy?"

Martha's mouth watered. It seemed so long since she had tasted candy. Not since Willis Tinsley had offered her the piece that day in May. There was never enough money for candy.

"Let's ask Mama." She started for the house, Ben following her into the kitchen.

Mama, a big white apron around her middle, was stirring potato soup on the stove. She looked up and frowned at Martha's question.

"Right away the first day here? Well, I guess you may go. But take Tina with you. And be back soon."

Pulling Tina between them, Martha and Ben started down the dusty road. She told them about the big cloud and the coyotes howling at night, and all the other hard-to-understand things which had happened. While she talked, a meadow lark warbled from a clump of wild plum bushes and a cottontail scurried through the weeds that lined the road.

The walk didn't seem long, and soon the three reached the store. After peering at all the candies in Mr. Tinsley's glass-covered case, Ben chose six pieces of peppermint.

"Now we'd better hurry back," Martha said when Mr. Tinsley had tucked the candy into a brown paper sack.

She glanced anxiously at the sky. She always worried about another wind cloud. A sudden gray pall had drifted over the late afternoon which seemed tinged with a smoky odor. Then Martha saw it toward the south — smoke and flames, rolling up faster than anything she'd ever seen.

"Prairie fire!" she screamed in terror, grabbing Ben's arm. "Look, over there!"

8. Prairie Fire

TONGUES OF ORANGE FLAME licked hungrily at the prairie grass which bordered Albert Tinsley's field of ripened spring wheat. The fire rolled in billows of angry black smoke. It was less than half a mile away.

In minutes the road streamed with horse teams and wagons, horseback riders, and men and boys on foot, carrying burlap bags and old quilts. The people pressed toward the fire, their shouts mingled with the snorts from the horses. As if by magic, plows appeared and strips of sod were overturned east and west of the store to build a fireguard.

Martha gripped the porch rail of the store tightly as she watched the flames and smoke roll steadily closer.

"Ben! Ben!" she screamed, spying her cousin near the fencerow that stretched southward toward the raging fire. "Ben, come back! We'd better go home!"

Ben turned and shouted. "I want to see what's going on, Martha! You hang onto Tina. We'll go back when the fire's out!"

The fire swept quickly over the wheat field, the air heavy with the sharp smell of burning grain. Beating the flames with wet sacks, the Mennonite farmers were pushed back inch by inch. Would the fire devour the Tinsley farm buildings and then sweep on to burn the store? Martha shuddered at the thought.

She hunted for Tina and found her huddled against the east side of the store, her blue eyes dark with horror.

"Come, Tina," Martha called quickly, "we must start back for our place. Our mothers will be worried."

Meekly Tina let herself be led away from the building while Martha held tightly to her small cousin's damp hand. As they started for the road, Alice Tinsley's pink and gold figure flew toward them, her hair awry and tangled with sweat and dirt.

"Oh, Martha!" she cried. "Our fields are burning, and the fire's almost to the barn. Is our house going to burn — and the store too? Everything we own is on this farm! What's going to happen to us?"

"Alice —" Martha gulped. She tried to speak calmly. "God is taking care for you! See, there are many men and boys working to stop the fire. Is Willis safe?" she asked anxiously.

"Oh, yes. He's with Mama," Alice said, her hands trembling on Martha's arm. "Look over there! What are those people doing? They — they are starting a fire close to the house! Is that helping?" she screamed, horrified.

Martha saw someone pumping water from the well

as men and boys dunked gunnysacks into the water. They had started a backfire, burning away the grass several yards south of the house and store, and beating the flames out with wet sacks. The prairie fire couldn't cross the burned strip, and this would save the store and living quarters.

"See, Alice? They're keeping the fire from spreading to the house, so you will be safe."

"But everything we own —" Alice began again, and gasped.

The barn was blazing now, the shooting flames piercing the pale blue sky. Hot sparks winged in every direction, and horses whinnied in terror. Martha saw a small group of Mennonite men huddled together, their lips moving. She knew that they all were praying.

She hoped Alice would trust God to take care of things. But, of course, Alice and her family seldom went to church. Maybe they didn't know about God. Or did He belong only to Mennonites, as Gerta said? But even Jake said he no longer believed.

Suddenly a faint breeze stirred, lifting the damp strands of hair from Martha's face. The wind was turning to the north, so the fire would advance no more. God had answered!

Martha watched in wonder as the pile of ashes which had once been a huge barn faded from black to gray to pale wisps of nothing.

The men, faces blackened by smudges of smoke, came back now, their battle against the prairie fire ended. They stood in small clustered groups as they wiped soot-stained beards with dirty blue handkerchieves and chattered.

Martha overheard Elder Warkentin's high-pitched voice above the others.

"We will all come back here after the ashes are cold and rebuild our friend Tinsley's barn. Then we will each bring a few bushels of our Turkey Red wheat. . . ." His voice droned on and on.

Martha rushed back to Alice, "Ach, isn't it wonderful?" she burst out half in English, half in Low German.

Alice clutched at Martha's sleeve again. "What did he say? What did he say? I don't understand your German, you know."

"After the ashes are cleared away, we will help your father build a barn. And when it is done, we all bring of our wheat to help make up for the crop your papa lost!"

A wan smile lit Alice's tired face and she squeezed Martha's hand. "I don't know what we would have done without you Mennonites. You *are* my friend, Martha. You're the dearest —"

Ben was there suddenly, his freckled face split into a wide grin. "This is the most exciting country in the world. Am I glad we came here! Come on, girls. We had better get back to the farm."

Martha couldn't help thinking what Jake would have said: "Crops burned up, barn in flames; who needs a land like this?"

9. Reenter: Gray Fox

"Martha, today you must take lunch to Papa in the field," Mama said one afternoon when the dishes were done and stacked hot and clean on the pantry shelf. "The plowing has been hard, and the days long. Even Prince and Nelly sag under the strain."

Martha looked up from her sewing. Even though her cousins were here, she still had to sew quilt patches. "But Papa is in the upper field, and that is almost a mile away!"

"Who says your legs can't carry you?" Mama chided. "You climb up on the mulberry trees and you play hide-and-seek all over the pasture. Ben can go with you, and the road will be only half as long!"

Ben grinned at her. "You haven't shown me everything your wonderful new land has, Martha?"

"Have you heard the coyotes at night? Ben, when

you've seen one strip of prairie, you've seen it all," she said with a slow smile. She knew there were many things Ben hadn't seen; perhaps if he did, he wouldn't think this country was so great. Jake had seen them and had gone away. But maybe he wasn't as full of adventure as Ben.

Mama had baked a panful of crusty sweet rolls. She wrapped some in a clean tea towel and placed them in a wicker basket. Then she filled a tin pail with coffee and jammed the lid on tightly.

"Carry it carefully so the hot coffee won't scald your legs. Ben will help you," Mama said briskly. "Now hurry!"

In a few minutes Martha and Ben were on their way. Ben swung the bucket of coffee easily while Martha carried the rolls and a battered tin cup.

The bold blue September skies still bore the bright glint of summer, and warm clods of plowed earth between their toes crumbled with each step. The fields were brown with dead cornstalks, and a stiff breeze blew over the tall prairie grass across the road.

Ben was full of chatter as usual. He could cause excitement to race up and down Martha's back at anything. Nothing seemed to dampen his spirits. She wondered if anything ever would.

Papa plodded behind the plow, his heavy feet planted firmly on overturned sod with every step, clucking patiently to Prince and Nelly and wiping the sweat from his ruddy face. He paused when he saw the two of them coming toward him.

"*Na,* this is a good excuse to sit down and rest," he called out. "The horses are glad for the rest too. I see you brought rolls and coffee."

He dropped the reins loosely over the ground and seated himself in the horses' shade. Martha dutifully handed the lunch to her father and watched silently as he ate.

Ben raced up and down the furrows, stopping to scoop up a fat white worm now and then, or watching a butterfly winnow down to cling to a strip of warm sod. Sunlight hammered on the freshly turned earth, and purple and red shadows flickered with movement.

Suddenly Papa pulled himself to his feet. "Well, the rolls are all gone, and the coffee almost, and I've had a good rest. Now I had better finish plowing so I can harrow and then plant the wheat for another season. Last year our harvest was good. The Lord blesses and provides."

Martha picked up the wicker basket and coffee pail. "Jake said God had forsaken the Mennonites when they left the comfortable steppes of the Ukraine and came to America," she said slowly.

Papa passed a grimy hand over his forehead and replaced his weathered straw hat.

"Ach, that Jacob never learned from God! If he would accept Jesus Christ as his Savior, he might see things differently. Jesus is our Lord and our Guide. He led us here!"

There it was again. Papa's faith. There were still so many things she didn't understand.

Ben came, grabbed the pail from Martha's hand, and started back across the fields, with Martha following him.

"Hui, this is great, Martha!" he shouted, jumping over the richly turned loam. "I'm having the time of

my life!" He rushed ahead for a few steps and paused to wait for her.

They had gone perhaps half a mile when suddenly Ben screamed. Martha panted up beside him as he sagged to the ground, clutching his left leg.

"I didn't see it until I stepped on it," he groaned, his freckles pasty white.

"See *what,* Ben?" Martha asked. Then she saw the rattler slither into a clump of dried pigweed and she shivered.

Quickly she knelt down as he pulled up his trouser leg. The fang marks looked ugly and dark red, and the flesh was already growing puffy.

"Ach!" she cried. "Oh, Ben, rattlesnakes are p-p-poison. Didn't you know that?"

"What — what shall — we do?" he said in a ragged whisper.

"Do?" Martha echoed. "I'm sure — I don't know!"

She stared fascinated at the purplish spot on Ben's leg. What could one do on the prairie — miles from a doctor — *except die?* Was Ben prepared for this?

"Ben —" she faltered, "have you ever let Jesus into your life?"

He stared at her, and then a slow hesitant smile broke over his white face. "Yes, back in Russia. No need to wait for danger to do that. Martha, am I going to — die?"

Martha shook her head fiercely and heaving sobs wracked her small frame. And Papa was so sure God had led them here!

A shadow fell across Martha's face and she looked up quickly. There stood the tall, black-haired Indian in the faded red tunic, eyes steely and sober. Martha relaxed. Gray Fox was back!

When Ben glanced up, he screamed. "Oh, *Gott im Himmel!* God in Heaven, I worship Thee!"

Martha laid a quick hand on Ben's shoulder. "Ben, this is Gray Fox. He is our friend, and he'll help us. Do as he says and let him do what he has to."

The Indian knelt down. Swiftly he drew out his knife and cut a small X over the fang mark, then pressed his lips over the cut and sucked out the blood and spit it out. Snipping a piece of thong from his belt, he tied it tightly above Ben's wound. After awhile he looked up.

"Snake bite not bad anymore." Then, with a sudden movement, he was gone.

Ben let out his breath slowly. "Whew! So that was an Indian? He didn't seem fierce, did he?"

"Not Gray Fox! He's our friend. Most of the Indians have settled down on the reservation. It's like Jake says, though. We took away their land, so we must be careful. But Indians are smart. They know things — things we don't know!"

"Hui! They know more than that stupid brother of yours. Jake thinks this land is terrible. Well, I like it."

Red color surged over Martha's face. Who was right, Ben or Jake? She didn't know who to believe.

10. Chitchat

SCHOOL WAS TO BEGIN IN MID-OCTOBER after the fall plowing and wheat sowing, for everyone had to help put the Turkey Red wheat to bed. Martha looked forward to school, for Ben and Tina would remain and go to school with her for awhile. The Mennonite children still attended the little sod schoolhouse which was taught by Mr. Andreas Fast, and it would be good to see Gerta and the others every day, even if Gerta was bossy.

Martha sat on the rope swing one afternoon under the mulberry tree and dreamed. Ben had gone to Morton with Papa on business, and Tina was taking a nap.

Growing restless, Martha jumped from the swing and watched it dally and stop. Then she walked slowly to the east side of the house and flung herself on the bank of wild grass. She braided strips of the prairie grass to pass the time.

Suddenly she spied Alice Tinsley marching boldly up the lane, and Martha jumped up and flew to meet her.

"Ach, Alice, you come to see me?" Martha said. "I was not knowing what to do, and I'm so glad!"

Alice smiled. "Glad in not knowing what to do?" she teased. "Martha, Martha, we'll have to teach you to speak a respectable English. Well, I've never been to see you, and Mama said I could stay for an hour today. Soon we'll be back in school and won't see much of each other."

Martha hung her head. "That's so. Where do you go to school? We speak so much German —"

"We drove to Cottonwood Crossing every day last winter, but the county has built that new white frame schoolhouse over on the corner, you know. It's to be called Clear Ridge. It has real blackboards, and there's a bell in the tower!"

"You speak just English in your school?"

Alice laughed again. "Of course! Don't you?"

"Uh, we talk German always at home," Martha said, her cheeks reddening, "but we start to learn a little bit English already in school."

"I understand next year you'll probably all join us at Clear Ridge. They're making a law that everyone must attend public school."

"But I can't very good talk English or read one line of it," Martha burst out anxiously.

"I'll help you. You'll learn fast, I'm sure."

The two girls had walked slowly up the lane, and Martha led her visitor to the shady side of the house where she had been playing. They sat down on the narrow strip of grass.

Martha tucked her long dark blue dress snugly around her bare ankles.

"Ach, that would be nice. I like school so very much."

"Just think! We could be together every day," Alice said gaily.

A small frown settled on Martha's forehead. She liked Alice very much. But was it right to love her as much as Gerta? After all, Alice wasn't a Mennonite, even if she was more pleasant and not as pushy as Gerta. If Jake were around she could ask him.

Down the road a wagon creaked and horses snuffled. It must be Papa and Ben coming back from Morton. As soon as the wagon stopped in the yard, Ben hopped to the ground and landed beside the two girls in one big jump. He leaned back on his elbows and grinned.

"You don't know what a good time I had in Morton!" he said, and Martha was surprised at how well he spoke English.

Alice bent forward eagerly. "What did you do, Ben Goertz?"

Ben sat up and chuckled. Then he almost bent over double with laughter. Finally he caught his breath.

"Hui, it was so funny. I waited on the wagon seat while your father was in the store. An Indian squaw waddled up beside us, took down the papoose from her back, and set it down beside the door. Pigs were roaming around, searching for food. A hungry sow came along, sniffed the skin covering the baby, and thought it might make a good dinner. She rooted it over and started grunting at the baby's toes. The baby screamed, and your father came running out of the store and fought off the hungry pig and picked up the papoose. Indians appeared like magic. When they found out what happened, the Indian mother insisted on giving the baby to your father. Martha, you almost ended up with an Indian sister! Your father had a hard time trying to turn her down."

Alice and Martha laughed too — Alice most of all. Then she grew quiet.

"Know what I think, Ben?" she said softly. "The Indians won't forget this. They probably even followed you all the way home without your knowing it."

Ben and Martha looked at each other, remembering Gray Fox. It might be true at that.

Alice went on. "They'll fix a sign here on your farm and be your friends for life."

Martha shivered a little. If Alice was right, then Jake was wrong. Indians weren't always wild, wanting revenge. Gray Fox wasn't. He had been kind to her and Ben. Now Papa had been kind to them. Wasn't that how it should be?

A happy feeling scooted through her and she laughed again. Alice was going to teach her how to speak English and someday they would be in school together. If only they could be friends, too.

11. Off to School

MARTHA TIED THE DRAB WOOL SCARF over her long braids and patted her clean white apron which covered most of the front of her dark blue dress. Mama wouldn't let her wear the pink sunbonnet because the other girls had none.

"Mama, is our lunch ready? Where's my Bible?"

Mama picked up the tin syrup pail from the table and handed it to her. "All ready. The rye bread is fresh, and the sorghum molasses thick and sweet. Eee, here's your Bible, just where you left it on the big chest last night. Do you have your slate?"

Martha crinkled her nose. "I left it at school. We were not to erase the sums Teacher Fast wrote down for us. Mama, I like school so much. I hope I never have to stop going to school to learn!"

Ben laughed. "Someday you'll grow up and marry a Mennonite boy and be done with school."

She made a wry face as she picked up the syrup pail and her Bible. "Ach, you're a slowpoke, Ben Goertz. You'd better hurry or we'll be late."

They set out briskly down the lane and hurried to the road. Already the gray skies were sodden with moisture, and it looked like rain again. There had been a lot of rain that fall, and although the wheat grew lush and green, mud squished underfoot on the road.

Martha, Ben, and Tina tramped along the soft ruts and stopped in front of the Harms farm. Gerta stepped out of her A-shaped house just as Martha swung her lunch pail impatiently in an arc. Across the road Peter Wiebe barreled out of his front door with a merry shout.

"Hui! Can you guess what I saw yesterday? A real Indian!" he yelled.

Ben and Martha glanced at each other. They knew Gray Fox. "So? What happened?" Ben asked.

"Papa and I rode horseback down by Cottonwood Creek, and there we saw the Indian trying to catch fish in the water. He wore a band around his black hair and a faded red shirt. I guess those poor Indians don't know better. Papa would never let me wear a red shirt."

"Or Elder Enns either," Ben laughed. "Gray Fox," he mumbled to Martha.

"What did you say?" Peter asked.

"Nothing."

"What did the Indian say, Peter?" Martha prodded.

"Oh," Peter burst out laughing, "he couldn't speak Low German and I couldn't speak Sioux. So we grunted at each other. He gave me some wild berries

64

after pointing to my pocketknife on a chain, which he wanted."

"And you gave it to him?" Ben asked.

Peter fidgeted. "I had to. You don't want the whole lot of us to get scalped, do you? Better do as they say, Papa says."

Gerta drew herself up proudly. "Indians are heathen. They are not protected and kept by God the way we Mennonites are!"

"But Papa says," Peter said, "that God loves everybody, and someone should tell them that Jesus loves them. Maybe they could become Christians."

"Christians. Impossible!" Gerta said testily. "And you'd let them come to our school and learn to read and write? Is that what you want?"

"Oh, you needn't worry," Peter replied with a short laugh. "They can't understand Low German. Besides, we'll always speak Low German here in America."

"Do you really think so?" Gerta said with a toss of her dark head. "We won't have to learn English?"

"I hope not."

"Ach, but we will," Martha said. "Alice Tinsley told me we'll be going to Clear Ridge School next year."

"That would be stupid," Gerta grumped. "We Mennonites are to be kept separate. You know that."

"But we'll be doing many of the things our English neighbors do," Ben said. "And they'll do some of the things we do."

"Like raising Turkey Red wheat," Peter said.

"Oh, you don't know everything," Gerta snapped. The group had reached the sod schoolhouse and

Martha marched into the dim, musty building and placed the dinner pail on the corner shelf. Teacher Andreas Fast sat hunched behind his desk, his wire-rimmed glasses perched on the tip of his thin red nose, looking very wise, which Martha was sure he was. To think he received all of $20 per month just for teaching school!

Before long, he rang the handbell and then opened the morning session with a long prayer. Then came a period of singing, followed by Bible study, geography, arithmetic, and penmanship. At noon Martha shared the molasses sandwiches with Ben and Tina.

School was such a wonderful place. Martha tingled down to her toes with the thought of being able to learn so much.

As classes ended for the day and the teacher pronounced the closing prayer, the skies opened and rain poured down in sheets. Long flickering flashes of lightning and drum rolls of thunder added to the gloom of the steady downpour. Rain seeped through the sod roof and dripped on Tina. She began to whimper.

Just then Papa came after the children with the team and wagon, splashing down the muddy road in the driving rain. Martha's kerchief grew soggy and she clutched an old quilt over her damp head when she settled onto the wagon floor.

Finally the wagon clanked up the drive, wheels sinking deep into the thick mud. When the wagon creaked to a stop, Martha jumped from the tailgate and ran through the blowing rain into the house. The long brick oven was still warm from bread-baking, and she hung her wet kerchief and apron over the back of a ladder chair to dry.

Ben had promised to help Martha feed the ducks and geese huddled in the flat sheds, but he lingered outdoors. Just as Martha started for the door to go to the sheds, Elder Enns rushed in.

"It's the schoolhouse!" he panted in Low German. "The sod walls have caved in from the rains, and now we'll have no more school!"

No more school! Martha's heart sank. No more learning to read and write and work sums? No more learning the English language? She couldn't believe it. Dragging herself to the barn, she opened a bin and scooped up a bucketful of corn and scattered a few grains to the hungry ducklings. They clustered noisily around her long skirts and clamored for more, but she hardly noticed. She remembered what Peter had said about the Indians, and how Gerta had been so set against their coming to school. And now there was no school for even the Mennonite children. God protected Mennonites no better than other folks. The schoolhouse had collapsed. Maybe God did love everyone alike, the way Peter's father had said.

Tears stung Martha's eyes and she wiped them away with one corner of her still-damp skirt. If there was to be no more school, how could they learn to read the Bible and to work numbers and everything they needed to know? Or learn the English language so they could go to Clear Ridge School next year?

After she tossed another handful of corn to the ducks, Ben burst into the shed.

"Here, you go into the house now, Martha. I'll finish the chores."

Without a word Martha plodded through the mud back to the house and went into the kitchen. She

poured a dipperful of water from the tin bucket into
the wash basin. She rinsed her hands and face, then
dried herself on the rough towel which hung behind
the door. She got out the cracked plates and carried
them to the table. Life would go on, even though she
could no longer go to school.

Papa and Ben came in from the barn, cheerful as
ever. As though nothing had happened. Of course,
Jake would say this was another stupid thing the
Mennonites had done: built a sod schoolhouse instead
of one made of stone or wood.

"Na, Martha," Papa said with a twinkle in his eyes
as he wiggled his neatly trimmed beard, "you children won't be lucky enough to get out of going to
school after all."

Martha whirled around, balancing a cup on a
saucer in one hand. "But the schoolhouse has caved
in, Papa. Elder Enns just said so. Didn't you hear?"

"Yes, I heard, Martha. But while Ben and I were
in the barn, Franz Buschman rode up. He says on
Monday the doors will open for you all at Clear
Ridge. Teacher Fast won't be your regular teacher,
but he will go up every day and teach the Bible for
all those who wish, so you will still learn about God's
love and His Son, Jesus Christ."

Martha's spine tingled. Why, it meant she could
see Alice Tinsley every day! And Alice had promised
to help her with the English language. She wondered
if someday someone would also learn to speak the
Sioux Indian language so the Indians could learn of
the Gospel.

Right now, the fragrance of fresh-baked bread
lingered in the kitchen, and the bubbly sound of

gravy in the pan made her mouth water. She was suddenly very hungry, and she thumped the rest of the dishes onto the table.

Ben eyed her sharply. "Monday we will begin to speak English, Martha. But we'll still eat in Low German. When do we eat?"

She began to laugh so hard that she shook all over.

12. Sunday Morning

FALL STOLE OVER THE PRAIRIE with a riot of color as the low hills in the east dipped and swelled, black with newly turned earth, yellow with stubble, tawny brown with cornstalks, and green with the first faint promise of newly seeded Turkey Red wheat.

Martha and Ben raced along the tan pasture, picking up cow chips and stacking them neatly into piles. They would be used for fuel when winter arrived. Already they had gathered broken, discarded railroad ties along the tracks, driftwood in the shallow creek beds, and dead plum brush, piling it all behind the tool shed. Even weeds had been chopped for kindling, and old straw was bound into bundles for the baking oven.

Every weekday the children had marched boldly two miles away to Clear Ridge School, where they learned English, arithmetic, spelling, writing, and history. But today was Saturday, and there was much to do.

Ben's father had returned from the Dakotas where he had bought a homestead claim and the Eli Goertz family would move there before cold weather set in.

"I'll miss you, Ben," Martha said, her arms loaded with chips. "It's been good to have you here with us."

Ben nodded. "I've had lots of fun too. I only hope our new home will be as interesting and exciting. Guess our old friends from the Ukraine would never have believed about the Indians and the prairie fire."

"Or that you were bitten by a rattler," Martha added. "I'm glad you've liked it here, Ben. Jake hated it. He said this was wild country. But —" Her voice trailed off sadly, remembering her brother.

"Someday he will come to his senses and be glad your family came to America."

"But we're so poor," Martha protested feebly. "Times are hard, and there's so much work and so little money."

"One day," Ben told her with assurance, "your Turkey Red wheat will feed the world! And you'll be *proud* to be a Mennonite of Kansas."

Martha smiled a little at that. Ben always made her feel good. As much as she loved Jake, just before he left home he had not been able to make her feel at ease as Ben now did.

Martha and Ben piled their chips into a crude wooden wheelbarrow which Papa had built of scrap lumber, and carted their loads behind the tool shed. Someday maybe there would be other means of finding fuel to heat the house, and no smelly cow chips to drag home.

Even now, things had begun to change. The ne̶̶
McCormick reaper had already moved in last summer, brought in by some of the Civil War veterans,
and even the Mennonites grew excited about the pros-
pect of doing away with the slow scythes, cradles, and
sickles. The carefully built shocks of wheat could be
stacked; and next year the threshing machine would
take over the old threshing stone.

Neighbors like the Tinsleys, who had settled earlier,
were friendly, and offered plenty of advice. They had
fought grasshoppers, floods, and blizzards, and now
they could help the Mennonites settle in their midst.
Alice Tinsley told Martha that her father would long
remember how the neighbors had helped fight the
prairie fire and had saved his house and store, and
had even replenished the grain he had lost by bringing some of their own precious hoard of wheat. Most
of all, he couldn't forget how they had left their busy
fieldwork and rebuilt his barn — without pay.

Martha thought about some of these things the
next morning while she combed her long hair and
plaited it into braids as she got ready for church.

Services were conducted in a squat wooden building, once used as an immigrant house for incoming
settlers. Martha clutched her Bible tightly against her
as the wagon lumbered down the dusty road. Driving
past farms scattered along either side of the road, the
Friesen and Goertz families saw the freshly built
adobe houses of new Mennonite settlers, the well-kept
farms of the Civil War veterans, and the lush pastures
dotted with horses, sheep, and cattle.

When the wagon clanked through the shallow ditch
that led to the churchyard, Martha nudged Ben's arm.

"Look, Ben! The Funks from our old village in the Ukraine. I wonder when they arrived in Kansas."

"More and more Mennonites have left the old country," Ben told her. "I guess we'll see many of our old friends before long."

The wagon pulled to a stop, and Ben and Martha catapulted from the wagon box and hurried across the short grass to the church building. Martha was glad Mama had let her wear the pink sunbonnet. The old kerchiefs were fast growing out of style.

As they hurried toward Amelia Funk, who stood forlorn and alone by the church door, Martha smiled. Amelia had always been quick and chirpy like a sparrow. Her brown dress and long thin neck made her seem more birdlike than ever.

"Amelia!" Martha cried, throwing her arms around her old friend from Russia. "I didn't know you had come until I saw you as we drove up."

Amelia lifted sorrowful eyes to Martha. "Martha, we've had a long, tiring journey and I'm so weary. Everything's so big and lonely and hard over here. Coyotes howling in the night! Why did we leave our lovely vineyards and pretty gardens and cozy villages behind? This Godforsaken —"

"No, no, Amelia," Ben broke in quickly, "Kansas is not forsaken by God. He is with us here as in the Ukraine." He spun around and stalked away. Martha and Amelia watched him go.

"I felt the same when we first came," Martha said with a short laugh. "Well, you're here, and now there's Gerta — and — Alice. Why, I'm finding more and more friends all the time. Look, it's time to go into the church for services. I think Mama will let us sit

together today. It's been so long since we've seen each other."

"Alice? Who's Alice?" Amelia asked finally.

"Why, she's an English neighbor. She's very nice."

"Is she a Christian?"

Martha blinked hard. "Why — why, I don't know. She isn't a Mennonite, if that's what you mean."

"Same thing," Amelia snorted and hopped up the step.

The people settled themselves on the board benches and the services began. At first they rose to sing *Nun Danket Alle Gott* ("Now Thank We All Our God") after which Elder Enns walked to the front. He read the Scripture text: "They that sow in tears shall reap in joy. He that goeth forth and weepeth, bearing precious seed, shall doubtless come again with rejoicing, bringing sheaves with him." Then he began a long sermon in a sonorous, solemn voice that made Martha drowsy. To her it meant only one thing: they had brought precious Turkey Red seed from Russia with them, and they would expect a good harvest. And the tears — well, Jake wasn't willing for tears and other dangers. Yes, that's what it meant. The fields of Kansas were, after all, no different from the fields of Judea.

Suddenly she was startled as Elder Enns said, "We must not forget God's promise to Jacob when He said: I Am with thee, and will keep thee in all places whithersoever thou goest." His voice was like thunder, and the verse lodged in Martha's mind and lingered there.

The service was over and the audience rose to sing *Die Gnade Uns're Herr Jesu Christi"* ("The Grace of

Our Lord Jesus Christ"), and then they were dismissed with the benediction.

After visiting with friends, and inviting the Funks over for dinner, Papa clucked, and Prince and Nelly plodded slowly down the road toward home. Sparrows, perched on a low stone fence, whirred away as the wagon creaked closer, and a mother bobwhite with a flock of chicks crossed the road almost in front of them, scurrying into the dried brush like brown leaves before an autumn wind.

Martha thought, "Ben and Tina will leave soon, but the Funks have come, and I have Gerta. I'd like to have Alice, too — if it wasn't wrong. And maybe Jake will come back someday. I hope so."

13. Dried Bones on the Prairie

ONE EARLY SATURDAY MORNING in late October Martha scrambled out of bed and slipped into her clothes. She had lain awake for a long time after the rooster crowed to announce the dawn. Last night the coyotes had howled at the full moon, sending shivers down her back. She hurried down from the loft and glanced out the window. Stars still hung pale in the pink morning sky. Already she heard the snuffling horses in the barn and knew Uncle Eli was harnessing the team.

Her uncle was planning to drive about twenty-five miles away to buy a plow, and he had asked Ben and Martha to go with him.

"We must start early," he'd said. "It's a long way."

Now Martha set the thick plates and cups on the table for breakfast. She knew Ben was helping with early morning chores by lantern light.

Shortly after breakfast, dressed in her warm winter coat with a blue, knitted scarf tied snugly over her head, Martha hopped onto the high wagon seat between Ben and Uncle Eli. It would be a long, tiring drive. Good thing Mama had packed a lunch.

As Uncle Eli clucked, the team clanked slowly down the driveway. The air was chill and the autumn mists were rising. Then the sun turned the little pink clouds in the east into warm gold and the chill was gone.

At first Martha and Ben chattered about everything, but after a few miles they fell silent. The wagon jogged on and then left the well-defined road to follow a narrow, winding trail that led up and down the gently rolling hills. They crossed narrow streams lined with sharp outcroppings of rock ledges. Now and then a stone house, stark and brooding, sat alone in a scrub of brush; sometimes there were only two or three limestone blocks jutting out of the tall grass.

They finally reached the Hobbs ranch where the plow was for sale. After Uncle Eli had loaded it into the back of the wagon, they stopped to eat their lunch under the trees and prepared to leave.

"We'd better go," Uncle Eli said tersely, stroking his bearded chin after they had finished their lunch and watered and fed the team. "It's a long drive back home."

Mr. Hobbs, the rancher, turned to them. "There's a shortcut if you follow the lower pasture and go around that hill up ahead. It will cut off at least five miles. It rejoins the trail beyond the third hill."

The wagon creaked as the horses jogged on. The sun hammered warmly on Martha's back and she pulled off her scarf. She leaned wearily against Ben and fell asleep.

Suddenly someone shook her and she awoke. "Look, Martha. See — over there!"

She opened her eyes sleepily and stared at Ben's pointed finger. The wagon had stopped by a draw. Several deserted covered wagons, their canvas tops rotted and slashed from the wind, stood grim and lonely with only bleached bones of teams and human skeletons lying stark and gruesome in the shadows of the draw.

"What — what happened?" she gasped, fear clutching her spine.

"Settlers on the move, probably wandered off the trail and became lost," Uncle Eli said solemnly. "Or maybe they were poisoned by bad drinking water. Or Indians," he added as an afterthought.

"But Indians would have stolen the horses," Martha defended them, thinking of Gray Fox.

"Anyway," Ben said, "it happened long before today. I guess maybe no one has ever found them, hidden away like this. I'm sure it can't happen again."

"What makes you so sure?" Martha demanded. She was tired, and the sight of the dried bones disturbed her. She couldn't forget her brother Jake's fears. "Why are our parents so certain this is where God wanted them?"

Uncle Eli clucked to the team and the wagon lumbered on. Then he cleared his throat.

"God sees ahead as we cannot. He knows what is best. Sometimes we must travel through dark valleys to get where He wants us to be. But even though we had fine farms and villages in Russia, we were becoming aware that the Czar was planning to take away the freedom which had been promised to us."

"And what did that mean, Papa?" Ben asked.

"It meant," Uncle Eli said, pausing and stroking his chin, "that we stood a chance to lose title to our land and property, and our freedom of worship. And our young men would have had to join the Russian military. Broken promises. Our 'Eden' was tumbling around us, and many Mennonites all over the Ukraine and Crimea in south Russia saw this and decided to leave while they had the chance. Perhaps if we had remained in Russia we might have wound up like these poor wanderers of the wagon train. We would have met our deaths too. Especially death to our Christian freedom."

Ben tweaked Martha's wheat-colored braid. "See? What did I tell you? Things are safer here now, Martha. And in time everything will work out for good."

"Do you really think so, Ben?" she cried. "Do you think Jake could have been wrong?"

"Wrong? Jake didn't have a sense of adventure like you and I have." Ben laughed.

"Nor faith in our God," Uncle Eli added solemnly.

The three fell silent as the wagon creaked on. Martha's hopes rose. "God's promise to Jacob: 'I will go with thee.' I wish I could tell Jake about it. I wish Jake would come home," she thought for the thousandth time.

14. Thrills

"MARTHA, MARTHA!"

Alice Tinsley rushed up to Martha on the school ground and threw her arms around her, hugging her tightly.

"What's the matter, Alice?" Martha asked when she could catch her breath.

"Oh, you'd never guess. Next Friday, President Hayes and Mrs. Hayes are visiting the state capital, and we're going to go by train to see them!"

"How marl-evous!" Martha said. She still struggled with the English language. "Our President of the America States!"

"Oh, but guess what else, Martha?" Alice went on, her eyes shining. "Mama said I could choose one of my friends to go with us, and I decided on my very best friend — you!"

"Me?" Martha echoed. "Me go to see the President? But —" Best friend? But Alice *couldn't* be her friend. She wasn't even a Mennonite!

"Now don't say you can't go. Papa has already talked to your father, and he has said you could go. The train leaves early and we'll spend the day and come back before dark. There'll be parades and bands and everything. Won't it be exciting?"

"Ex-citing?" Martha savored the new word. "Ach, yes, it will be ex-exciting! And Papa says I can go!"

The two girls hugged each other again and danced into the school house. It would be hard to keep her mind on her sums today. The "times tables" and the "sevens" were the hardest. Martha could hardly remember what seven times eight was, and today she would be sure to forget.

Ben and his family had left for South Dakota so she couldn't share the exciting news with him, although she knew he would tell her it was much more thrilling than the time Count Tolstoy had visited the Ukraine and ridden down the village streets of Pastwa. But, of course, that was long before either Martha or Ben were old enough to remember.

Mama washed and starched Martha's second-best dress and ironed its stiff ruffles carefully. She even found a scrap of black velvet ribbon for a bow at the neckline. Mama also lengthened and brushed Martha's winter coat which had been turned and made over from an old one Mama had once worn in Russia. Mama had found time to stitch a new brown velvet bonnet of leftover scraps from a sofa pillow she found in the bottom of the old trunk in the loft.

Early Friday morning Mama pronounced Martha ready to go. "But be careful you don't step on the hem of your coat. I made it a little bit long because you are growing so!" She helped Martha onto the wagon so Papa could drive her to the Tinsleys, and Martha settled back on the stiff seat as comfortably as she could without crushing her starched ruffles.

Papa eyed her shrewdly and chuckled. "You look so nice, Martha. Just so the President won't want to take you along to Washington with him!"

"Ach, Papa!" Martha protested. "Why, he won't even see me in all the big crowds."

"Well, you're dressed as nice as anyone. That's how we did it when Count Tolstoy came to Pastwa. We painted fences, cleaned our yards, dressed up in our best clothes —" He paused, remembering.

They reached the Tinsley farm just in time. The family carriage was already tied to the hitching post in front of the house, ready to leave. The ride to the train station in Peabody would take barely an hour.

Soon they were on the train, with Martha and Alice sharing a seat near the window in the crowded coach. The train whistled, and with a clang of bells and a rumble of steam, it was off. At first Martha and Alice chattered excitedly, but after awhile they grew quiet.

Bumping along the rails, Martha grew sleepy, and she leaned her head against Alice's shoulder and drowsed.

Someone shook her awake. "We're coming into Topeka now. Better brush the cinders from your eyes."

Martha stirred sleepily and blinked. She could see the state capitol dome in the smoky haze of the morning and the city streets blurring past the windows.

And then the train moved slower and slower, and with a great burst of steam it shuddered to a stop.

Mr. Tinsley placed a hand on Alice's shoulder. "We are hiring a cab to drive us to the parade route. There you two girls must watch Willis while your mother and I go to the newspaper office on business. Later, we will pick you up. But don't let Willis out of your sight for a minute!"

"Oh, Papa, you know we won't," Alice promised.

Martha added, "I'll hold his hand the whole time."

The cab clattered down the hard cindered street and stopped to let the two girls and Willis off on the corner in front of the big bank building.

"Remember," Mr. Tinsley called out as the cab began to move, "you wait for us right there, and don't move."

Alice grabbed Willis' left hand and Martha held tightly to the other. Carriages and buggies rattled past and crowds began to gather. A chill wind had whooped out of the north, causing Martha to pull her coat tighter around her throat.

Willis grew restless and jumped up and down, almost thumping on Martha's toes.

"What's a President?" he asked suddenly, tugging at Martha's coat sleeve.

"A — a President? Ach —"

"A President is a big man," Alice said with a patient sigh.

"As big as a house? Does he have whiskers like Martha's papa? Does he take giant steps? Do Presidents learn Bible verses like Martha does?"

"Oh, hush, Willis!" Alice snapped impatiently. "You talk too much."

"The President is just — just a plain man, like anyone," Martha said.

"Then why does everybody want to see him?"

Alice sighed again. "Oh, Martha, what shall we do with Willis? He — well, he's just going to nag us to death!"

Martha thought quickly. "If we had some candy—"

"That's it! You hang onto Willis and I'll dash into that shop over there —" Alice's words floated after her as she flew in the direction of a nearby drugstore.

Martha stared after her. It just wasn't possible that she, Martha Friesen, a Mennonite girl from far-off Russia, was stranded on a big city street, hanging onto the wriggling hand of a little boy! Oh, what would Papa and Mama say if they knew? She should never —

There was a sudden blare of trumpets and then a band of musicians tramped in step down the street, playing marching music. Willis jumped up and down in rhythm, screaming at the top of his lungs. Was he afraid of the thundering drums, the raucous horns? Tears stung Martha's eyes and she clung more tightly to Willis' arms. Why didn't Alice hurry back with the candy? She couldn't manage Willis another minute.

Just then a big black coach drawn by four plumed black horses clopped slowly down the street. In the front seat sat President and Mrs. Rutherford B. Hayes. The crowd shouted and whistled, and the President lifted his tall silk hat and bowed right and left.

Suddenly the horses stopped, and the President stepped from his coach. With a beaming smile he

moved onto the sidewalk and picked Willis up in his arms.

"Look here, young man," the President said, "why are you afraid? I'm your friend."

Willis stopped screaming and a big grin spread over his face. "So you are a plain man, like Martha said. Do you learn Bible verses?"

"Bible verses? But naturally. Everyone needs God. And who is this Martha?" the President's deep voice boomed as he set Willis down again.

Martha felt red color surge over her face, and she gulped. Willis grabbed for her hand in the crowd and pulled her forward.

"This is Martha, and she's our best friend."

President Hayes tipped his hat and bowed. "So nice to meet our best friend, Martha!"

He took her hand and kissed the tips of her fingers. Then he whirled around and was helped back into the seat by a liveried footman, and the coach moved on.

Martha froze. She forgot about Willis for a minute, thinking about what had just happened. Friend. She couldn't be friends with people who weren't Mennonites, could she? Yet the President of the United States had kissed her fingers! Then she felt Alice's hand on her arm.

"Martha? What was that all about? You look like you've been struck by lightning."

"That?" Martha blinked. "I guess — it was —ex-excitement. . . ." Her voice trailed off lamely She was still stunned.

Papa and Mama would never believe this, and maybe Jake wouldn't either. But Ben would! And the Tinsleys would talk of nothing else for days. And Alice had called her "best friend."

She sighed happily. At least she could tell Jake there were other things in Kansas besides Indians and snakes and prairie fires and tornadoes.

15. The Blizzard

WHEN MARTHA AMBLED OFF TO SCHOOL that morning in late November she noticed the sky. It was turning to slate and darkening to black near the horizon. But the breeze was mild, and now and then slivers of sunlight needled through the gray clouds.

She stopped at Tinsleys for Alice and the two girls hurried down the road toward school together. Mary Buschman and the Wiebes and Gerta Harms had probably gone on ahead.

Squaw winter had come and geese had flown in V-shapes toward the south. The tall prairie grass drooped like forgotten tufts of whiskers on a bald man's face on the slope of the tawny hills.

Martha and Alice chattered as they hurried down the hard-packed wagon road.

"I still can't believe that President Hayes talked to you," Alice bubbled. "It took so long at the store when I went after the candy. There were so many people —"

"I was too little to remember when Count Leo Tolstoy came to Pastwa, but this I will remember always," Martha said with a happy sigh.

Alice laughed. "Well, you should! If your cousin Ben were here, I'll bet he'd carry you all the way to school. He thought so much of you, Martha."

"I miss Ben," Martha said wistfully. "But I miss my brother Jake even more. I wish Jake would come back. Only —"

"Only what, Martha?"

"Jake thought we should have stayed in Russia. He would have been satisfied with Count Tolstoy." She laughed a little.

"Oh, but you Mennonites did right to come here. Papa says his field of Turkey Red wheat is the finest he's ever seen. And to think you brought it along from your Ukrainian steppes."

"It can stand very cold weather too," Martha said. "Even if it should snow hard."

Alice glanced at the sky. "Yes, snow can come any time now. It's getting darker, and we'd better hurry before it begins to snow."

"Do you think it will snow, Alice?"

"It looks like it."

The wind turned suddenly and keened and whooped out of the north over the prairies. Every yellowing leaf on the clump of cottonwoods beside the Clear Ridge schoolhouse whirled in a wild dance, and the first pellets of snow began to fall in sheets of hard, sleety crystals. The girls ran up the path and flung themselves through the schoolhouse door.

Miss Grimes had stoked the barrel stove, and it threw shafts of warmth over the room.

"Looks like you girls made it just in time," she said, taking their coats and hanging them beside the stove. "Not everyone is here this morning. Perhaps some of the others have turned back. But we'll make the best of it together, won't we?"

The wind died down, but snow continued to fall, soft and light, the noiseless cat feet of winter. It settled on the woodshed and penciled the bare cottonwood branches with thin white lines. All morning the snow fell softly, and when the wind rose again and howled around the corner of the schoolhouse, the teacher looked worried. Gerta and the Wiebes hadn't come after all.

"I think we had better dismiss school," she said anxiously. "If you all start out now, you'll make it home before the blizzard strikes."

Martha and Alice bundled up warmly, and Miss Grimes wrapped their scarves snugly about their faces. Together they started out in the snow, which already lay like a white fluffy blanket over the road. It had filled the wagon ruts and smoothed the road over as if by a cold hand. Snow blew into their faces as they plunged down the silent trail.

"Can you see where to go?" Martha panted, her hands growing stiff in spite of her knitted gloves.

"Oh, yes, just follow me. We'll make it," Alice said, pushing ahead through the deepening snow. "I've done this before."

Slowly, heavily, the two girls plunged on, with the icy wind in their faces and pellets of snow blowing into their boots.

Once Martha fell down, but Alice pulled her to her feet. "We've got to keep going," Alice muttered.

But the snow and the wind clawing at Martha's tired body were too much, and she stumbled and fell again.

"Just let me—rest. I'm so—tired," she whispered.

This time Alice grabbed Martha's shoulders and dragged her along the road.

"Don't do that again, Martha," she said sharply. "We have to keep going."

"Is it far?" Martha cried.

"I — I don't know! But we can't stop."

"Are we lost?"

Alice shook her head wildly. "Of course not, you silly goose. Don't be such a fraidycat."

A deep wooden culvert spanned the road, and Alice pulled Martha down into the ditch with her. Snow seeped into their boots and sleeves as they ducked down into the wide opening.

"Look, Martha, this is a cozy place to wait until the storm is over," Alice said. "Crawl in after me. We'll curl up together. See? It's not so cold here."

Martha blew on her cold fingers and crawled into the culvert after Alice. She shivered although she could no longer feel the sharp icy wind.

Wind continued to whip around the culvert and howl like a white-sheeted ghost. Alice arranged their coats over their legs and they lay back and talked. Huddled together, it didn't seem so cold.

Alice, who had been the cheerful one, suddenly asked a worried question: "Martha, just what if — what if — we don't get out? What do you think would happen?"

"Happen?" Martha thought awhile. "We could die. The Bible says something about a kernel of wheat falling into the ground and dying, and if we believe on Jesus we will be made alive again, like the way wheat sprouts. Papa told me about it once. He said that 'whosoever shall call on the name of the Lord shall be saved,' but I never really have. Now I think I understand what Elder Enns said in church a few weeks ago. He said that those who 'sow in tears shall reap in joy,' but I wasn't listening very hard."

Alice nodded. "I understand about the wheat. But what *did* he mean?" she asked anxiously.

"I think he meant that if we're sorry for our sins we will find joy in His forgiveness. Yes, I think that's it. Ben once said, 'Don't wait for danger to do it.' But now —"

Alice fell silent and both girls were quiet. Martha grew drowsy.

Then Alice spoke. "Martha, you Mennonites came to Kansas with practically nothing. Yet you've given us so much, like helping us put out the prairie fire, and then rebuilding our barn, and giving us your precious wheat. And now you've offered something else: how one can find peace with God!"

Martha thought about it and blinked the sleep out of her eyes. She shut her eyes tightly and prayed to let Jesus take over her life.

Suddenly she wasn't afraid anymore. God had taken away her fear. She only wished she could have seen Jake once more. She kept her eyes closed and waited. Her hands and feet had grown numb and she was growing sleepy again. She didn't hear Alice praying.

Out of the howling wind another sound came — the rumble of a wagon and snorting of horses coming over the frozen, ice-swept road.

Alice shook Martha, and the two girls scrambled out of the culvert and staggered through the snow-filled ditch.

"Papa!" Martha screamed. "Papa, here we are!"

The team stopped. Seconds later, Papa picked her up and carried her into the wagon, and then he went after Alice. The wagon bed was piled with straw, but there were mounds of warm covers and some hot bricks to warm their feet, and Martha and Alice snuggled together again.

The ride home seemed very short. In spite of the bitter cold, the Turkey Red wheat would survive, and so would the girls' newfound faith!

16. Christmas Surprise

CHRISTMAS WAS APPROACHING. Back in the Ukraine, Mama would have spent days baking *pfeffernuesse* — mounds of tiny cookielike morsels — and sugar cookies to hang on the tree. There would be secret trips to the store for mysterious gifts, wrapped in stiff brown paper. And each Christmas Eve there would be plates on the table, filled in the morning with nuts and candies and fruit.

But now, of course, they were too poor for anything like that, atlhough Mama had baked the usual gallons of the little "peppernuts," as Alice called them, and flavored them generously with molasses.

Weeks ago Martha had begged Grandma Wiens' help in spinning balls of wool yarn which she had dyed bright yellow with the roots she had found growing along the cottonwoods. Secretly she had knitted a warm scarf for Papa and a pair of mittens for

Mama. On an impulse she knitted a jaunty cap with thick earflaps for Jake — just in case he came home.

How much she would have to tell him if he came. But, of course, he wouldn't come. She had hoped and prayed for so long, and still he wasn't home. While knitting needles clicked busily in her fingers, she memorized the piece she would speak at the church Christmas program. It was called *"Heilige Abend"* — "Holy Night" — and she liked to think of that wonderful night so long ago when angels sang and the star shone, and Mary and Joseph cuddled the baby Jesus in the old barn. She wondered if maybe the barn was made of adobe, like their house, and she smiled a little, knowing Jesus had been poor too.

"Please, Jesus," she prayed as her fingers flew, "it would be so nice if Jake came home. But if it's asking too much, just let him be happy — wherever he is!" She wiped a tear from her eyes with the corner of her blue apron and sighed.

Tomorrow was Christmas Day, and the Mennonite families would gather at the immigrant house-church for an all-day celebration. There would be sermons and pieces and singing. At noon everyone would bring out cold ham and stewed wild fruit and fresh-baked two-story yeast rolls called "zwiebach," and they would all eat together. After the meal Gerta and Amelia and Martha would join the other children in singing, "O Come, Little Children, O come one and all," and they'd giggle and try to keep on pitch. Mama said one didn't need *things* to keep Christmas.

The piney fragrance of evergreen lingered everywhere, for Martha had decked the doors and windows with sprigs from the fir tree in the pasture, trying

to foster a holiday feeling. Outdoors, the snow had all but melted, leaving only white and tan splotches over the prairie like the hide of a Guernsey cow. A cold, hard sunset touched the sky as frost snapped among the young mulberry branches.

On Christmas morning after Papa had stomped in from the barn with pails of foamy milk, and Mama had cooked a big panful of cornmeal to eat with heavy cream and molasses, Martha crept from the loft and warmed her toes by the long stove. She pulled on her warm, black knitted stockings and slid into the high-button shoes. The buttons were hard to manage when one's fingers were stiff from the cold.

Papa washed up at the tin basin while Mama poured the cornmeal into a thick white bowl. Martha finished brushing her wheat-colored hair so Mama could braid it neatly after breakfast. She wanted it extra nice for Christmas.

"I'm glad the sky is clear today," Papa said, wiping his hands on the towel that hung behind the door. "It will be a long, cold drive to church."

Martha hid her gifts shyly under her apron. After they were seated at the table and Papa had prayed the long Christmas morning prayer, she took them out quickly and shoved Papa's yellow scarf toward him while she dropped Mama's gloves beside her plate.

"Merry Christmas!" she cried, trying to sound gay and breezy.

"Eee!" Mama's eyes filled with tears. "Why didn't I remember to put plates out! But I had nothing to put on them this year. . . ." Her voice faded. She got up and opened a drawer and drew out a new blue apron. It had rows of red cross-stitching across the bottom.

"For you, Martha," she said simply.

She gulped quickly. "Thank you, Mama. And hasn't it been a fine year?"

"Eee? Fine year?" Mama echoed. "I don't see —"

There was the quiet sound of a door opening, and Martha stretched to look past Papa's big form. Framed in the doorway stood a tall, thin figure — somehow familiar, somehow strange.

"Jake!" she squealed, jumping to her feet and running to throw her arms around him. "Ach, Jake, you did come home!"

Jake looked taller, older, and wiser, somehow. He squeezed Martha tightly, then hugged Mama and Papa, who had rushed toward him at the same time.

"Welcome home, son," Papa said huskily. Mama cried, hugging Jake again and again. Then she hurried to fetch another bowl and scooped cornmeal into it.

Jake took off his shabby coat and sat down at his old place at the table. He looked around.

"Lucky I got a ride those last few miles — on an Indian pony. Everything's the same, yet different," he said with a new note in his usually sullen voice.

"God heard our prayers and sent you home. Let us thank Him," Papa said. By now the meal was nearly cold.

"Oh, Jake, I'm so glad you're home," Martha said, almost too excited to eat. "But you were wrong about — about Kansas not being the right place. So much has happened, and —"

Jake grinned broadly, spooning more molasses over

his cornmeal. "You are right, Martha. I found that out shortly after I left. There are dangers in the big cities too. Once I was mugged and robbed, and another time I was nearly run over by a horse-drawn trolley car. And I was often cold and hungry —" He paused awkwardly for a moment. "I also found out that God is the same everywhere. That He leads us where He wants us to be. I gave Him my life one night when — well, it was a bitter experience when I lay too sick to move and yet afraid to die. I thought I'd never live through it, but He helped me. Some wonderful folks named Danner took me in. They were not Mennonites, but they love God the same as our people do. They took care of me and showed me the way to find Jesus and then gave me a job. Yes, God helped me. His love is stronger than the Mennonites or the cloud or the snakes."

"Me, too," Martha whispered, remembering the blizzard and how she and Alice had huddled together inside the culvert.

There was so much to tell about the prairie fire, the rattler, Gray Fox, and meeting the President. Martha was breathless when she finally ran out of words.

Papa and Mama pelted Jake with questions, and suddenly Jake snapped his fingers.

"I mustn't forget to tell you, Papa. This man Danner is a miller and he is very much interested in the Turkey Red wheat. He'll buy much of what our Mennonites will raise next year, and you won't be poor too much longer. They say this hard winter wheat makes the best bread."

Martha smiled to herself. She'd known all along

they had been wise to come to America, hadn't she? Well, maybe she had doubted, but even if she hadn't known, God had. She jumped up and hunted for the cap she had knitted for Jake and thrust it into his lap.

"Merry Christmas, Jake."

He laughed and laughed and hugged her tightly to him. He was her happy, fun brother again. "No one will take me for an Indian, anyway," he chuckled.

"Wait until Gray Fox sees you!" she said, laughing for sheer joy.

"So that's the friendly Indian who gave me a ride on his pony when I was too tired to move on. I told him who I was, and he said you were his friends. And, Martha, I see you're still the same girl you were when I left. You wanted America — and Kansas especially — to be right for us, but I didn't. Well, let me tell you. Be a Mennonite, Martha. But also be an American. Most of all, always live like a Christian!"

Martha knew what he meant because that's what she wanted. She had Gerta and Amelia for her friends, but she could have Alice too. And now there was Jesus. The sowing and the reaping. It all went together with faith and trust. Like the Mennonites and Turkey Red wheat.

Suddenly she glanced at the tall German clock which hung on the wall. "Ach, look at the time!" she cried. "We'll have to hurry to get ready for church."

And she brought the comb to Mama and waited for her to braid her long hair.

THE
PICTURE BIBLE
FOR ALL AGES

Do you have ALL SIX
books?

Vol. 1—CREATION: Gen. 1 to Ex. 19.
All the action from "In the beginning"
to the Flight . . . in pictures!

**Vol. 2—PROMISED
LAND:** Ex. 20 to I Sam.
16. Moses, Ten Com-
mandments, wander-
ings, fall of Jericho.

**Vol. 3—KINGS AND
PROPHETS:** I Sam. 16
to I Kings 21. Shows
David and Goliath,
wisdom of Solomon.

**Vol. 4—THE CAPTIVI-
TY:** I Kings 21 to Mal.
Covers the Babylonian
captivity, prophecies
of Jesus' coming.

Vol. 5—JESUS: Mt. to John. Dramati-
cally shows the birth, teaching, mir-
acles, final triumph of Christ.

(Cont.)

LIVING UNAFRAID. Do you have fears? Most people do—and this book tells about some who overcame their fears by applying an age-old truth: "Thou alone, O Lord, makest me to live unafraid." Read their stories . . . gain encouragement from their victories. By Dr. Charles W. Keysor, director of publications, Asbury College.   86439—$1.25

PEBBLES OF TRUTH. Poems for all Christians, on topics of basic interest: the love of God . . . faith . . . repentance . . . forgiveness . . . salvation . . . obedience . . . fellowship . . . freedom . . . rejoicing . . . loyalty. By Dr. William S. Stoddard, pastor of Walnut Creek (Calif.) Presbyterian Church. Illustrated.   86371—$1.25

THEIR FINEST HOUR. Engrossing biographies of people whose dedication to Christ still inspires those who share their faith. Some names you will recognize . . . others, not. For instance: William A. "Devil Anse" Hatfield. His conversion ended the most publicized feud in America's history! Photos. By Charles Ludwig.   82917—$1.95

THE PROPHET OF WHEAT STREET by James W. English. In hard cover, it was the choice of six book clubs! English, former editor of Boys' Life, tells the story of William Borders, a southern black Northwestern graduate who returned to lead Atlanta's black church to revitalized faith, improved housing, new self-respect.   72678—$1.25

ALCOHOLISM by Pastor Paul. Encouragement for alcoholics, and all who are concerned about them—a pastor tells how God helped him beat the bottle. Although well educated and respected, the author found release not through his own efforts alone, but through the help of God . . . and those who offered their strength.   72629—$1.95

O CHRISTIAN! O JEW! by Paul Carlson. A member of Christians Concerned for Israel, Pastor Paul Carlson traces the progress of prophecy . . . from God's covenant with Abraham to the miracle of modern-day Israel. He presents a seldom-seen side of Jewish-Christian relations to help Christians better understand Jews.   75820—$1.95

B

LET'S SUCCEED WITH OUR TEENAGERS by Jay Kesler. An eminent authority, the president of Youth for Christ International, offers a new understanding of the age-old but desperately new problems even the happiest of families must face: coming of age, discipline and love, peer pressure, drugs, alcohol, tobacco, the Church.   72660—$1.25

BEFORE I WAKE. Are you ready to face death—your own death, or the death of a loved one? Both philosophical and practical, this book by Pastor Paul R. Carlson presents the Christian view of the nature and destiny of man, draws on doctors, psychologists, lawyers and morticians to help one face grief, make a will, arrange a funeral.   86454—$1.50

CHRISTIANS IN THE SHADOW OF THE KREMLIN by Anita and Peter Deyneka, Jr. Why can't the rulers of Russia banish faith? They've closed churches, taught atheism in the schools —yet a vital (if unorganized) church remains. How can it be? Come and learn as the authors talk with Russian students, workers, professional people. Photos.   82982—$1.50

THE EVIDENCE THAT CONVICTED AIDA SKRIPNIKOVA by Michael Bourdeaux. This book places its reader at the side of a young Russian girl on trial. She chooses imprisonment to the abandonment of faith in a story that challenges ALL Christians. (Bourdeaux is a worker at London's Center for Study of Religion and Communism.)   72652—$1.25

HOW SILENTLY, HOW SILENTLY. Joseph Bayly's modern-day fables and fantasies lead to spiritual discoveries: The wise computer's treatise on whether or not Man exists. The boy who arrives at college with shields of pure gold and returns home with shining shields that nobody recognizes as brass. The Israeli, in America at Christmas—who was he?
73304—$1.25

LOOK AT ME, PLEASE LOOK AT ME by Clark, Dahl, and Gonzenbach. Two church women tell about their work with the mentally retarded, how concern led them through fear and revulsion to acceptance and love—also to the discovery that often behind the facade of physical unloveliness waits a warm and responsive personality.   72595—$1.25

C

D